HAPPY STORIES FOR ANIMAL LOVERS

Leisa Stewart-Sharpe

Anna Shepeta

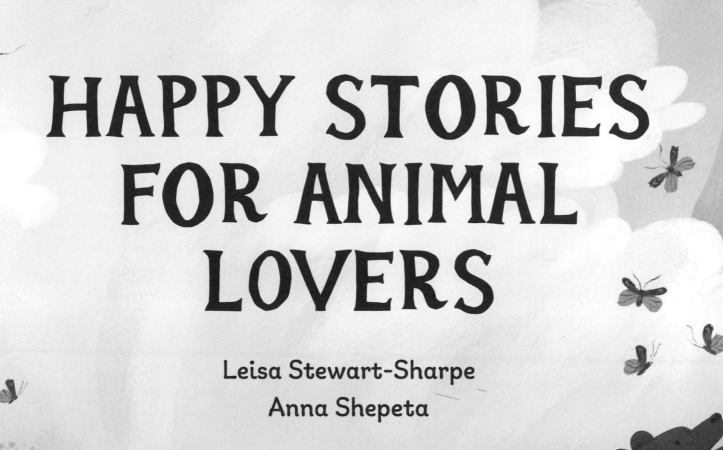

IVY KIDS

Welcome, wild things . . .

Is it night where you are? Do stars twinkle and wink in a velvety
sky, as you snuggle down in your bed, the covers pulled right up
under your chin? Or perhaps it's daytime and you've found the
perfect patch of sunshiny light, to settle down in for a story?
Go on then, have a final wiggle, and a wriggle, and we shall begin.

Because no matter whether it's day or night, it's always a good time
for a story. And the very best stories you'll ever hear—are true.
They're unfolding right now, in nature all around. Animal stories
so unexpectedly wonderful they'll make your heart beat wildly.

You won't be able to help it. Your eyes will grow wide,
and your mouth will twitch into a smile, as you
discover animals happily doing what animals do . . .

Wandering
Wallowing
Soaring
Diving
Climbing
Snacking
Building
Playing
And even . . . peeing.

Well, I did say it would be wild!

Best of all, these stories will make you glad of this
magnificent planet and the amazing animals we share
it with. Because even though there are some eight
billion of us, there are *countless* more of them helping
to keep our planet in perfect balance. Which is why
now more than ever, we need to make just a little more
space for our animal neighbors. And when we do, we
might just find ourselves growing a little wilder too.

So, what are you waiting for?
It's time to read these stories aloud; to breathe
life into them so they can run and fly off the page.

Once upon a time, on a **WILD PLANET** . . .

The Wildebeest Wander
A story from Africa

Ears twitch,
tails swish,
hooves pound—
the wildebeest are on the move.

Nose to tail and shoulder to shoulder is the wildebeest way—
about two million of them swarm across east Africa's plains
each year. They head clockwise, like clockwork, from Tanzania to
Kenya, then back again—an epic journey as the wildebeest chase
the rains. For where there's water, there's grass.

But before the first raindrops fall, a newborn does . . . born into
the green grasses of Tanzania's south Serengeti plains. Then
along comes another, and another. It's February and it's raining
calves as thousands are born in a single day.

They teeter,

they totter . . .   then try again.

they tumble,

Within a few weeks, up to half a million calves have arrived.
They must find their footing fast, for no sooner are they born,
than their journey to find fresh grass to graze on has begun.

More than a million wildebeest weave and wind across
the plains, with hundreds of thousands of zebras and
gazelles zigzagging by their side.

Soon, the dry season is ahead, and so are the rivers.
Their banks are steep and sandy, and their waters altogether
SNAPPY as crocodiles eagerly open their jaws.
Who will be the first to take the plunge?

It's a leap of faith . . .

and the crocodiles LUNGE!

On and on the wildebeest wander, through the
golden grasses of Kenya's Maasai Mara nature reserve. Until finally
it's December, and they've returned to the plains where they were
born. A round trip driving the great circle of life. For the wildebeest
are the true kings of the Serengeti! They keep the grasses short,
so fewer fires spark under the hot sun. This gives trees a chance to
grow, bringing insects that feed the birds, and leaves to feed giraffe
and elephant herds. Hungry predators such as hyenas, lions, and
leopards then follow and pounce.

It has long been this way, as the wildebeest make this seemingly
endless journey. Yet the great plains are *not* endless; fences and
farms are now blocking the wildebeests' way. And so, in one special
place, the Indigenous Maasai people
rose up to tear the fences down.

Eight villages came together to create a wildlife reserve on their ancient lands, stretching across a vast area. It's a crucial wildlife corridor, connecting the Maasai Mara to the Serengeti for millions of migrating animals. They call this place Nashulai (Na-shoo-lie), which means somewhere the spirit of people and nature come together and sing a song. Now humans, livestock, and wildlife *share* the grasslands. And the "*gnu gnu*" bark of the wildebeest fills the air once more.

The Jungle Jewel

A story from Indonesia

I found a jewel in the jungle.
It is not bright. It does not sparkle.

It is gray and creased with saggy skin like a saddle.
It is a Javan rhino, but I like to think it's a *unicorn*.
Rare and rarely seen, but I know where to find it.
I watch as it tramples through the forest to find a puddle.
And when the puddle isn't large enough, it tramples it too.
That makes it much bigger—better.
Slowly it slips into the mud—lathering and slathering.

A ROLLING RHINO.

A good wallow is better than swatting at mosquitoes.
It turns its gray skin brown. Cools it down.

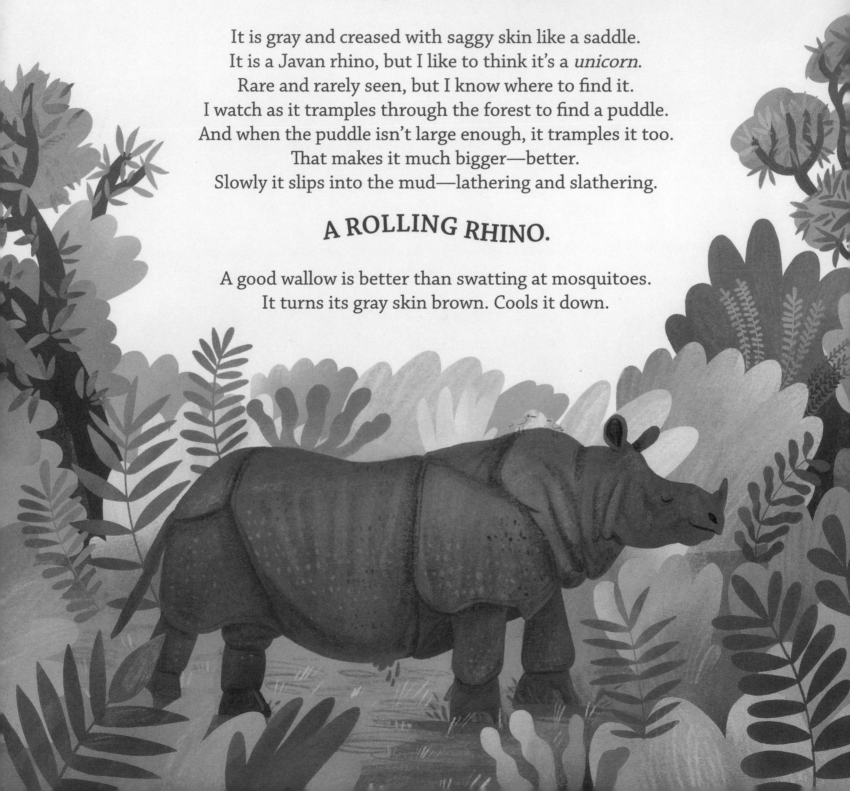

You won't find my unicorn in a zoo.
He is hiding in Ujung Kulon Park with some seventy
others. It is their only home—their only hope.
They are the last of their kind.

There are other jungle jewels here—marooned on Java,
an ancient island jutting into the Indian Ocean.
Where volcanoes simmer and gibbons howl.
Leopards prowl. Poachers too.

**They would like to take my unicorn's horn,
but we won't let them.**

We go with rangers, by foot, by bike, by boat, tracking down
poachers and taking their traps—laying our own.
But ours are only camera traps,
perfect for watching a **GOOD WALLOW**.

*Javan rhinos are so elusive, even the rangers who protect
them from poachers rarely see them, so they depend on camera traps
to be their watchful eyes. Sometimes those cameras capture the rhinos
doing what they love best—happily wallowing in ponds and rivers.*

Flying Back From Extinction
A story from Europe

"Kommt, kommt, Waldis, kommt, kommt!"

This is the call of a mother to her chicks, high up in a meadow on the Austrian Alps. It means: "Come, come, ibis, come, come." Except, unlike her brood, this mother *isn't* a bird—she's one of two *human* foster mothers to thirty northern bald ibis chicks.

These extremely rare birds haven't been seen in central Europe for almost 400 years, having gone extinct due to hunting and habitat loss. Then, in 2002, seven of these beautiful birds were unexpectedly found in the Syrian desert in the Middle East. Scientists saw it as a chance to turn back time for this species, bringing the northern bald ibis back to Europe and back from extinction.

For six months these foster mothers have been working day and night to hand-raise the ibis chicks, doing everything their mother would have done had they been born in the wild. The human foster mothers have . . .

. . . fed them, cleaned them,
talked to them,
played with them,
and cuddled them.

Now, as summer comes to an end, their final lesson is about to begin . . .

. . . it's time to fly south for the winter.

The ibis will spend the next month flying about 750 miles up and over the mountains, then down into a sheltered valley in southern Italy, just as their ancestors did centuries ago.

The journey won't be easy. The winds will be strong, and the weather can turn wild. And if that wasn't hard enough, how will they ever learn to fly when their mothers haven't got wings to show them?

Or do they?

The foster mothers fly ahead in little planes, calling to the chicks: **"Kommt, kommt, Waldis, kommt, kommt!"** And the chicks follow their instincts, and their moms, falling into a perfect V formation behind them.

The jet-black feathers around their necks ruffle in the wind, gleaming green and purple in the sun. And with their huge wings outstretched, the warm air rises beneath them . . .

. . . lifting them up, up, up, so they can fly.

The ibis will remember this flight for the rest of their lives—a journey they'll one day go on to teach their chicks, too.

As for their mothers, they'll always remember the happy spring and summer they spent helping these bald babies fly back from extinction.

As of 2024, fifteen human-led migrations have helped introduce over 200 northern bald ibis back into central Europe, giving hope to endangered migratory bird species everywhere.

Disco in the Deep
A story from the United States

In the deep dark reaches of the ocean, light is swallowed by the dark. The water's great weight presses down, hiding secret places, where strange things lurk.

Places

unmapped,

unexplored,

and unknown.

Then along comes . . .

A GREAT WHITE SHARK.

This master of the ocean has spent winter hunting seals in the warm waters around America's west coast. Like a torpedo, speeding up from below, he would break through the water, then bellyflop back into the waves.

Now spring has come, and along with hundreds of other great white sharks,
he's striking out on a mysterious voyage across the Pacific Ocean.

With satellite tags attached to his body, the shark swims
AND THE SCIENTISTS FOLLOW.

He swims farther and farther from land—about 1,240
miles—until the great white reaches a remote part of the
ocean halfway between California and Hawaii. A place
humans long thought of as an oceanic desert.
It showed *no* signs of life.

It turns out . . .

...WE WERE WRONG. This patch of ocean is an oasis.

Like submarines,
sharks dive

d
o
w
n

Into the inky depths of
the Twilight Zone.

Down here, beyond the reach of the sun, creatures shimmer and strobe. They're making their own light through bioluminescence to communicate and lure in prey.

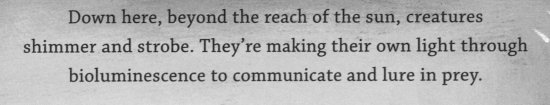

It's like a **DISCO** in the dark.

By day, they stay in the Twilight Zone some 1,600 feet down, and by night, they swim up toward the ocean's warmer surface waters to feed. And the sharks follow their every move, up and down, sometimes 150 times a day. Scientists think that the great white sharks dive to eat, but they can't say for sure.

It's little wonder scientists have named this mysterious place: "The White Shark Café."

Sharks led scientists to their secret café, and now the scientists are trying to discover all that they can about it so that they can protect it as a marine reserve, safe from fishing. Happy news not just for the great white sharks that come here, but for all mysterious creatures dancing in the deep.

The Hungry Bears on Moth Mountain

A story from the United States

"Grrrrr"

That's not a growl, it's a *rumbling* tummy.

It's high summer in the Rocky Mountains, and this hungry grizzly bear and her cubs are looking for lunch. At this time of year, an adult grizzly could eat up to ninety pounds of food each day (the same weight as eighteen chihuahua dogs), as it builds up its fat stores before winter. But so far, these bears have only found plants to eat. And with each tired step, daylight fades, and their appetites *grow*.

At her size, you might think Mom would be keen to scavenge on the remains of a big animal—perhaps something the wolves have left behind. But Mom has a different plan, as she leads her cubs up the mountains.

Climbing the stony slopes is like hiking in roller skates as loose rocks shift under their paws.

The cubs were promised lunch, but so far all they've done is climb!

They go **higher**, and **higher**.

Up the barren slopes, until they reach
the snow near the summit.

Driven by hunger, the mother bear hurries
ahead and begins clawing at the ground. Suddenly,
she buries her head in the rocks and emerges . . .

... with a mouthful of moths!

Moths?!

Starved, the cubs follow Mom's lead, digging up swarms of fatty army cutworm moths that they can smell resting below ground. The moths are much more satisfying to eat than plants, and give the bears the energy they need for hibernation. Mom could eat up to 40,000 in a single day.

In summer, army cutworm moths migrate huge distances, high up into these mountains. In the heat of the day, they shelter under the rocks, but when the sun sets, millions of them flutter into the night. Sweeping and swooping to forage in wildflower meadows farther down the mountain.

The moths will return to the rocky slopes at sunrise, where the bears will be waiting for them. The cubs will remember this precious place, just as their mother did, and will someday come back with their own cubs, too.

Some 50,000 grizzlies once roamed the United States, south of Canada. Today, around 2,000 remain. Grizzlies need plenty of space to wander in their search for food, a mate, and a den. But their range has been dramatically reduced as highways, towns, and railroads cut across the land. To help, government and conservation groups are buying up chunks of land to stitch the grizzlies' habitat back together, while also working with landowners so that bears and humans can safely share the landscape.

Built by Beaver

A story from the United Kingdom

Slow, slow the river's flow,
burbling along the bed.
Rippling over rocks
trickling past trees, when . . .

TIMBER!

A tree falls, then floats—
going with the flow down this Cornish river.
There's the tree feller now.
A busy beaver—stocky rodent of the river—
gnawing on another trunk.
He chisels with his chompers, when . . .

Splash!

Beaver and branch go into the river.
They sweep along with the current, when . . .

STOP!

A dam.

It was built by Beaver,
from mud and sticks and leaves and logs.
It makes the river pool to form a pond.
The perfect place to build a home.
He adds another log,
and his lodge is *almost* done.

A mound of sticks and mud
that'll keep his family warm all winter long.
But that's only half the story,
for the lodge reaches *under* the river.

Look, there are secret entrances to a cozy chamber.
His fortress even has a "fridge"—
a spot in the middle of the pond
where he's buried a stash of branches.

Perfect to snack on when the river freezes
and the forest sleeps.

Until then . . .

CRACK!

Another tree falls in the forest.

A beaver's work is never done . . .

Four hundred years ago the Eurasian beaver went extinct in the UK,
after being hunted for its fur and meat. Now, conservationists have
reintroduced this busy little builder to the wild. The beavers' damming
and tree-felling helps to widen waterways, preventing flooding and
creating beautiful wetlands that all of nature can enjoy.

Friends in Frozen Places
A story from Canada

The winter wind is blowing across the Gulf of Saint Lawrence off the east coast of Canada. Each gust gently nudges the ice floes as they bump and bunch across the ocean, like bright white pieces of a jigsaw puzzle. Yet something else is slowly gliding under the surface . . .

. . . the WHITE WHALES have come.

A pod of sixty belugas has arrived to spend winter in the gulf. They use hard ridges on their backs to break through thin sea ice and peek above the waterline—they're spyhopping. The belugas are as white as snow, gleaming in the weak winter sun.

All but ONE of them.

His skin is gray and speckled, and he raises a twisted tusk into the air.

He is a narwhal—best buddy to these belugas. And he's known as Nordet, sharing the same name as the winds that blow from the north where he comes from.

Although narwhals and belugas
belong to the same animal family,
they rarely socialize in the wild.

Narwhals spend winter *under* the thick sea ice much farther
north, while belugas head south where there are ice-free patches
so they can surface to breathe. Many years ago, Nordet became
separated from his pod. Alone in the icy water, he befriended
these belugas, and has been traveling with them ever since.

As if he was one of them.

A narwhal may not look or act the same as a beluga, but they've welcomed him into their family all the same. Belugas love to make friends and will "hang out" with boys or girls, young or old, sometimes hundreds of them—chirping and squeaking as they chat to each other. And now this narwhal has even been spotted joining in at playtime—happily bumping and brushing up against the beluga boys. He's a teenager now—nearly old enough to find a mate. If Nordet can make a match with a female beluga, scientists hope they might spy something magical one spring . . .

. . . **a narluga baby!**

Nordet was first spotted with his beluga friends in 2016 and has been seen by watchful scientists every year since. If he does go on to father a narluga—it won't be the first! In 1990 an Inuk hunter, a member of the Inuit people of Greenland, showed a scientist a strange skull. DNA testing proved it belonged to a narluga—born to a narwhal mother and beluga father. For the first time it was proof that narlugas exist, and that peculiar friendships are sometimes made in the most extreme reaches of our planet.

Eat, Pee,
Eat, Repeat
A story from China

**Here comes the panda
—giant of China's misty mountains—
backing into position.**

A bit more, little bit more . . .
What's this?
He's *reversing* up the tree!
Higher and higher, 'til his hindfeet are above his head.

A hand-standing panda.

Who'd have thought it.
Oh no, he's not, is he? Oh yes he is.
The hand-standing panda is now having
an *upside-down* pee.
Leaving his mark on the bark,
so the other wild pandas know:

"I was here"

Tree pee done, he goes back to doing
what he does best: bamboo munching.
Some ten hours and eighty pounds of it a day.

Eat, Pee, Eat, Sleep, REPEAT.
It's been a *very* busy day.

For half a century, people have worked tirelessly
to save the giant panda from extinction, and along the way,
this black and white bear has become a well-known symbol for
conservation. Its bamboo forest homes have been replanted, nature
reserves set up, and pandas have been carefully bred in captivity
then returned to the wild, so that today their numbers have almost
doubled from 1,000 in the 1970s to around 1,800.

What You Can Do

All the stories in this book have one thing in common, as well as starring happy animals, they're about how people are learning to give our wild neighbors a little more space to thrive. But you don't need to live near a giant panda or a great white shark to make more room for nature in your life.

Here's what you can do at home:

✿ Build a five-star bug hotel out of sticks and logs, pinecones, broken pots, bricks, or canes to help keep invertebrates (woodlice, spiders, ladybugs, beetles) safe and snug.

✿ Mix bird seed, or uncooked porridge oats, mild grated cheese, peanuts, sultanas, raisins, and mealworms, with melted suet and lard, then mold it into energy-rich fat balls that can be hung from trees or shrubs. They'll be especially appreciated in the winter when fatty food sources are harder to find.

✿ Be a wildlife watcher and search online for a local animal count you can take part in. These seasonal wildlife surveys help conservationists keep track of wildlife in the area and the health of local ecosystems.

✿ Get the whole family involved with an organized litter clean-up at the beach, park, along the rivers, or in the woods to help keep these wild habitats free from plastic.

If you'd like to find out more about any of
the animals in this book, there are a few ways you
can bring them right into your home . . .

❀ Follow the wildebeest migration online at *serengeti-tracker.org*
❀ Track the flight of the "Waldis" through the free Animal Tracker app
❀ Tune into the beavers on their live web cam at
cornwallwildlifetrust.org.uk/live-beaver-cam
❀ Shadow a shark, following their movements at *topp.org*

And don't forget, from the mightiest bear to the stockiest beaver, our animal
neighbors can't speak up for themselves. They are counting on us to stand up
for them. Now that you know more about these incredible creatures, why not
give them a voice, by sharing their stories with anyone who'll listen.

So go forth animal lovers . . . be free, be HAPPY, and above all
be a good neighbor on this wild planet we can *all* call home.

With thanks to the following scientists and conservationists for sharing their wild wisdom and for their tireless work standing up for nature. Dr. Randall Kochevar at Stanford University; Robert Michaud at the Group for Research and Education on Marine Mammals (GREMM); Nelson Reiyia at Nashuali; Helena Wehner at Waldrappteam; Alastair Driver at Rewilding Britain; the International Rhino Foundation; The Vital Ground Foundation; Erik Peterson at Washington State University.—Leisa Stewart-Sharpe

For my beloved partner, thanks for always being there and supporting me.—Anna Shepeta

First published in 2024 by Ivy Kids, an imprint of The Quarto Group.
100 Cummings Center, Suite 265D, Beverly, MA 01915, USA
T (978) 282-9590 F (978) 283-2742 www.Quarto.com

A CIP record for this book is available from the Library of Congress.

ISBN: 978-0-7112-8585-9
eISBN: 978-0-7112-8959-8

The illustrations were created with colour pencils
Set in Chaparral Pro, Giulia Plain, Moon Firefly

Designers: Myrto Dimitrakoulia and Holly Jolley
Commissioning Editor: Hannah Dove
Consultants: Sophie Stafford and Barbara Taylor
Production controller: Dawn Cameron
Art Director: Karissa Santos
Publisher: Georgia Buckthorn

Manufactured in GraphyCems, Villatuerta, Spain, SE052024

9 8 7 6 5 4 3 2 1